lion and blue

lion and blue

by *Robert Vavra*

paintings by Fleur Cowles

PREFACE BY THE PRINCE OF THE NETHERLANDS

REYNAL AND COMPANY
in association with
William Morrow and Company, Inc.
New York 1974

Printed in the United States of America.
  2 3 4 5 78 77 76 75 74

Library of Congress Catalog Card Number 74-10319

ISBN 0-688-61164-8

Design by John Fulton

In this book Fleur Cowles and Robert Vavra have shown us for the second time how beautifully they can make us human beings feel the strange and haunting impact that the artistic expression of a genuine love of nature has upon us.

Knowing that a great deal of our flora and fauna is in danger of disappearing, it is with a feeling of nostalgia that one looks at these wonderful pictures and reads the sensitive text.

I sincerely hope that many, many people will be moved by this poetic work of art and that the feelings this book inspires will make them value the wonders of nature that surround us.

The Prince of the Netherlands

Soestdijk, 1974

My lonely roars
echoed far
in a jungle
that was old
to me,
a lion
in the winter
of his years,
whose heart
had never known
spring.

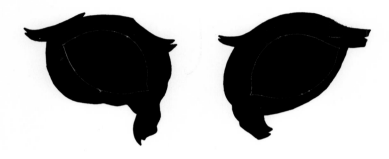

Until that afternoon
when in the darkness
of silent thoughts
my yellow eyes
were dazzled
blue.

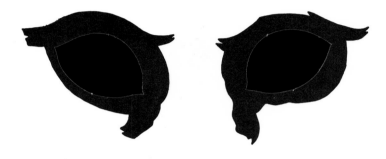

Suddenly blossoms
lit this dull stare
when you,
brilliant,
beautiful,
Brazilian
butterfly
drifted into
my life.

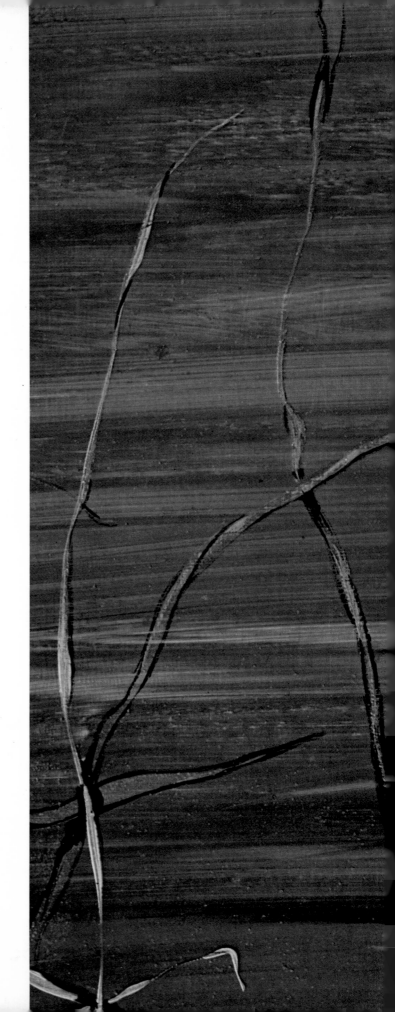

Blue became . . .
Blue was
my
love,
my
life,
my all around.

Happiness was
a spring and summer
that seemed could never
turn to
fall.
Though you told me,
'Someday,
Lion,
the time will come
when I will have to
leave you,
in search of
     the
       flower
         of
         the
         sun.'

Those thoughts made me
want to shut my ears
or roar away
a destiny
which threatened
our happy voyage
across
the sea of
love.

The other butterflies
clustered round my
head,
and off somewhere
I heard a lioness
call,

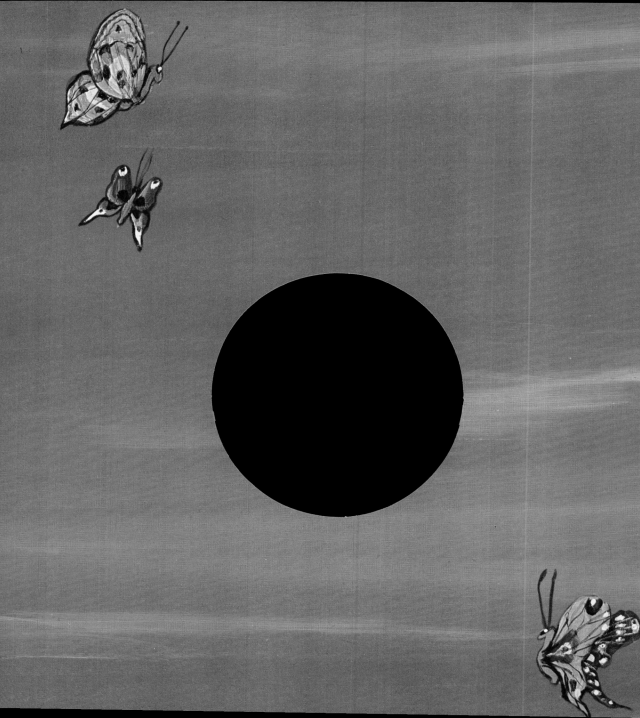

*Though my open
eyes
seldom left
your wings,*

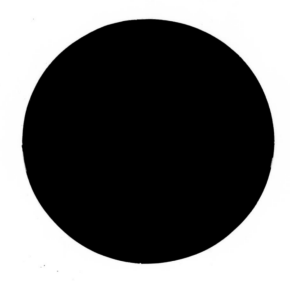

*one night you left
me,
Blue,
in search of
your golden
destiny.*

Then there was
no world for me.
Endless years
I awaited your
return.

*But our boat
drifted past
as empty as
my
heart.
And so my quest
began.
I sailed to places
far away.*

In search of
you
I wandered
far,
and all the while
I thought,
'Why could we
not have met
when the time
was right,
when youth had lit
my stars.'

'But yesterday is
over,'
whispered the
far-seeing giraffe,
'as tomorrow is
yet to come.'

'The only time
that is ever
right,'
rumbled the
wise elephant,
'is
n o w,
so make haste,
this journey of yours
is a one way trip
eternally.'

As I climbed the
grass
towards the clouds

'This flower is the leopard's,'
came the cheetah's voice,
'it sprang from the garden
of his soul.
You won't find the love
of which you speak
until your roots have grown strong,
grown deep.'

In the dark of
night
or in the flame of
morning sky
often hope would
awaken in my
heart
with the flashing
of blue wings.
But feathers covered
them
and not your
brilliance.

Then one day
on the plain's edge,
where the wind blows
fast and clean,
a wart hog came
trotting by,
a daisy in his
mouth,
and as he passed
I heard these words,

*'Lion
you have proven
your love,
now let the humble
daisies
set you
free.'*

White and straight
stood a daisy
proudly at the
field's edge.
'Come among us,'
beckoned the simple
flower.
And so I strode
through that meadow
of
honey and snow.
Then,
not the tawny lioness's
purrrrr
or the tides
of oceans
could take me from
my course.

But no blossom of
the sun was
there.
'The brilliant flower
you seek,'
lulled the daisies,
'is springing now
from your lion's
heart.'
And as rich pollen
covered me,
golden petals crowned
      my
      head.

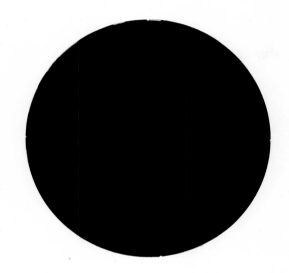

Centuries,
years,
days . . .
how many passed,
I don't know.
But born again
was I
when in the
evening sky
a dot of blue
appeared against
the moon.

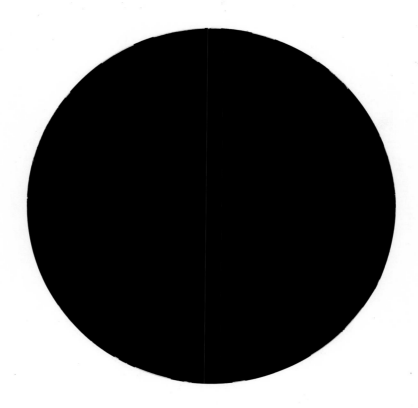

And as the sky

oranged

with break of day,

At last your voice
I heard,

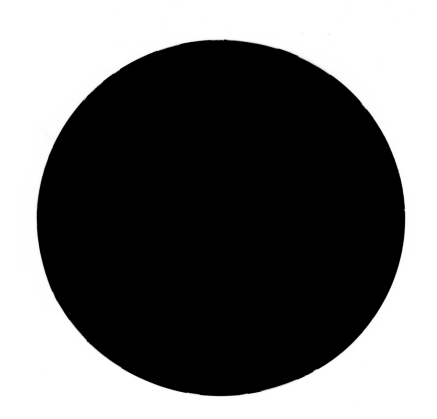

My
Golden
Maned
Flower
Hero
Of
The
Sun !'

And n o w . . .
Blue!
Blue!
brilliant,
bella,
Brazilian
butterfly,
again my life,
my all around;
                    is
                        you.

OWNERSHIP OF PAINTINGS